A Wish for Wings That Work

An Opus Christmas Story

Written and Illustrated by

Berkeley Breathed

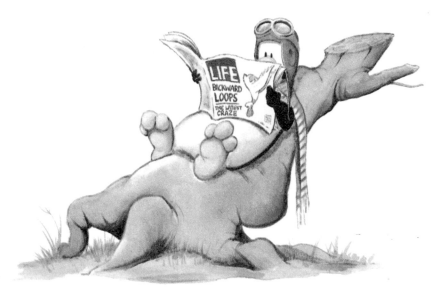

SCHOLASTIC

New York Toronto London Auckland Sydney

ISBN 0-590-46368-3

Copyright © 1991 by Berkeley Breathed.
All rights reserved. Published by Scholastic Inc.,
730 Broadway, New York, NY 10003, by arrangement with
Little, Brown & Company, Inc.

12 11 10 9 8 7 6 5 4 3 2   2 3 4 5 6 7/9

Printed in the U.S.A.   08

First Scholastic printing, November 1992

All men dream: but not equally.
　　　　　　—T. E. Lawrence (of Arabia)

It was a good morning to fly, even if it had come late and slow and so cold that a penguin feared his nose might freeze and drop off like one of the icicles hanging over the porch.

"Fly," Opus whispered to himself as he ran to the top of Duck's Breath Ridge at dawn to watch the snow ducks soar above. "Fly!" he whispered as he lifted his wings and waited to be swept up beneath the fading Christmas moon with the other birds.

But it was on mornings such as this that Opus's heart grew as cold as his nose. A penguin can surely say the word *fly,* but he cannot *do* it.

"A bird with wings that won't work!" Opus growled to himself. "What good is that? What good am I? I might as well have been born a snail. Or a slice of melba toast."

One day during lunch, he climbed the statue in the park and offered to share his last pickle with the pigeons. But they just rolled their eyeballs around and moved away. "It is not our pleasure," they sniffed, "to share pickles with birds whose wings do not work."

"If my wings will not lift me, I'll find something that does," thought Opus. He heard a man screaming on TV about a new product everyone should own called a FLAP-O-MATIC. Opus quickly ordered one.

When it arrived, he put it together and hoped everything was right, since the instructions were in a different language.

Opus carried it up to Vulture Gorge, strapped it on, and wound up the rubber band. Stepping to the edge, Opus looked down to the bottom three miles below. "Yow," he gulped. He sighed, walked back home, and spent the rest of the day cooking anchovy Christmas cookies, which wasn't nearly as dangerous.

And then Opus knew what he should do.

That night, he sat in front of his warm fireplace, considered his words carefully, and wrote an important letter:

> Dear Santa Claus,
>
> In the past I have asked
>
> for a scarf that would last.
>
> I have wished for new skates
>
> or some herring rum cakes.
>
> But since my wings sputter
>
> at those times they should flutter,
>
> I thought you should know
>
> I need wings that will go!

After mailing his Christmas wish, Opus congratulated himself that a penguin could be so clever, and he immediately went up to Duck's Breath Ridge to practice takeoffs.

"Santa Claus will be bringing me new wings," announced Opus to a passing snow duck. "I shall be flying on Christmas morning."

Christmas Eve soon arrived, and after leaving a note of welcome to
Santa Claus in the fireplace, the penguin whose wings would not work
tucked himself into bed. He burrowed down deep in his thick quilt, curled
his knees up to his chin, scratched his nose one last time, and, as a flock
of snow ducks drifted silently across the full Christmas moon,
closed his eyes.

"Fly," Opus whispered to himself just before falling asleep. "I'll be flying
on Christmas morning."

And then he was snoring.

Look.

There.

Above the hills.

Above the clouds.

A soft glow . . . growing brighter . . . closer . . .

What was it?

It was much too early for the sun.

Maybe it was a duck with a flashlight.

Listen: sleigh bells . . . ringing . . .

Ducks don't wear sleigh bells!

Why, it was him! Of course!

And with the thunder of hooves, Father Christmas himself burst through the midnight clouds!

On over the countryside Santa's sleigh swooped! And glided and zoomed and—

Wait. There was a bump.

A little thump.

Probably just some bumpy air.

Or maybe not.

Something was not right. A small piece of the harness had broken away. The reindeer flew on, but Santa's sleigh plummeted like a meteor toward the lake!

"Hello! Wake up! Emergency!" a voice hollered.

"Who's jumping about on my bed?" asked Opus, rubbing the sleep from his eyes.

A snow duck was holding a light over Opus and looking very upset. "Catastrophe! Calamity!" the duck hollered. "A considerable setback! Please! Follow me!"

Opus sighed and guessed that the milkman had slipped and gotten his head stuck in the porch railing again. He crawled out of bed and stumbled outside behind his midnight intruder.

"There!" said the snow ducks, and they pointed toward the dark lake. They lifted the little penguin so he could see better. Opus could just make out something: a lantern out on the water, a big man with a white beard, standing atop a sleigh that was teetering, rocking . . .

And sinking. Opus gasped in horror.

Down the snowy bank Opus scampered, a flash of black and white as he hit the water.

With a roar, a shimmering curtain of spray erupted behind the rushing missile. It held in the air for the longest seconds, catching the moonlight before falling.

Toadfrogs leaped!

Catfish jumped!

And Opus flew, strong and fast, through the icy water, a wonderful, roaring, graceful torpedo sailing through the darkness. He was swimming—and swimming, after all, is what penguins do best.

"There," whispered a snow duck from the water's edge. "Look there!" he said, pointing now, for something was moving toward them.

It was Opus, and he was pulling that great Christmas sled and all the toys through the freezing water with the reins in his teeth! There was great sloshing and frothing and—

Laughing?

Somebody was laughing. Out from the sleigh, a deep voice of good cheer drifted in over the water.

"Ho! Ho! Ho! Ho!" it rumbled faintly. "Ho! Ho! Ho! *GO!*"

Opus stumbled, exhausted, onto the dock. His arms ached, and it hurt to breathe. He noticed many eyes watching him, and he tried his best to straighten his soggy red bow tie.

He had brought the sleigh safely to shore. The reindeer were waiting there patiently.

The large man in the red suit approached, grasped his hand, and shook it gently. Santa's wide, pink face came down close, and his whiskers brushed Opus's ear. Opus noticed his kind eyes, one of which winked softly.

"I see no penguins here," Santa whispered, "whose wings only sputter. Tonight it was *courage* that flew yours beyond others."

He whirled, and with a snap of a whip and a hearty laugh, he and the sleigh sailed up toward the stars.

Opus awoke Christmas morning and stumbled sleepily to the door. But he found something besides the morning paper outside.

He rubbed his eyes in disbelief. There on his front porch—and spreading out across his lawn and down the street—were hundreds, maybe even thousands, of smiling snow ducks.

And each and every one wore a little bright-red bow tie.

Two of the ducks took hold of his arms and led him outside, where, slowly at first, and then faster, they all began running and flapping their wings.

"What's going on?" said Opus, but he already knew, for his feet weren't on the ground anymore. Over the street and above the houses those ducks carried Opus until they were way, way, above Duck's Breath Ridge.

Down below, people looked up, for they could hear a voice somewhere above the clouds. It was a penguin whose wings didn't work, laughing because he surely *was* flying on Christmas morning.